MOOSE,

GOOSE

and
Little Nobody

Words and Pictures by
ELLEN RASKIN

PARENTS' MAGAZINE PRESS
New York

E
C. 1

For my mother,
Margaret Raskin Shanske

One day a big wind blew.
Trees fell and a gas pump flew.
From somewhere a red roof
spun through the air
and came down with a
BUMP!

"What is that?" said Moose to Goose.

"It's a gas," said Goose,

"my good friend Gas."

"Hello, Gas," said Moose, "howdy-do."

"I am not a gas,"

said the little one in the red roof,

"I am a moose . . .

I think."

"Moose?" said Goose.

"You are not a moose."

"I am the moose," said Moose, "not you."

The little nobody cried and cried.

He had lost his mother,

he had lost his house,

and now he had lost his name.

He had nothing left in the whole world

but a red roof over his head.

"Don't cry," said Moose.
"We will find your name
   and your mother
   and your house."

"We will search the town,"
   said Goose.

Moose, Goose, and Little Nobody
searched the town until they found
a house without a red roof.
On it was a name.
In it was a mother.

"You are a lion," said Goose,
"my good friend Lion."
"Hello, Lion," said Moose,
"howdy-do."

"I am not a lion,"
Little Nobody cried,
"and this house is much too scary."
Moose and Goose agreed.

They ran and ran until they came
to another house
without a red roof.

"You are a phone," said Goose,

"my good friend Phone."

"Hello, Phone," said Moose, "howdy-do."

"I am not a phone,"

  Little Nobody cried,

"and my mother is not home,

  and this house is much too tall."

"Quite right," said Moose.

"This way," said Goose,

"I see a house

  with many mothers."

"You are a bus," said Goose,

"my good friend Bus."

"Hello, Bus," said Moose, "howdy-do."

"This house is much too big,"

Little Nobody cried.

"Maybe it is an apartment house,"

said Moose.

The apartment house drove away.

"I say," said Moose.

"I see," said Goose,

"another house

without a red roof."

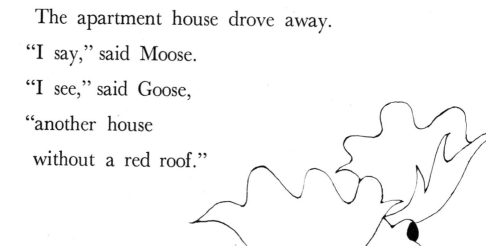

"You are a mail," said Goose,

"my good friend Mail."

"Hello, Mail," said Moose, "howdy-do."

"I want my mommy," Little Nobody cried,

but no one was home.

A pig came by,
then a fox,

then the mailman emptied the box.
"I am not a mail, a pig, or a fox,"
Little Nobody cried, "and this house
is too dark and empty."

"That way," said Goose," is a house
with a light in the window."

"You are a stop," said Goose,

"my good friend Stop."

"No, no," said Moose, "his name is Go."

"Stop," said Goose.

"Hello, Go," said Moose, "howdy-do."

"I am not a go. I am not a stop,"
  Little Nobody cried,

"and this house is much too flippity-flop."

"Quite right," said Moose
  as he caught the red roof.
"Poor little thing,"
  said Goose.

On and on they went.

The last house they came to

had no roof at all.

It was red

and just the right size.

"You are a snow," said Goose,

"my good friend Snow."

"Hello, Snow," said Moose, "howdy-do."

"I am not a snow," Little Nobody cried.

He jumped on the sign.

He stamped his foot.

"I am not, I am not a . . . oh!"

The sign tipped
and turned around,
right side up, upside down.
Little Nobody fell
into the arms of his mother.

"Little Mouse, Little Mouse,
my lost and found mouse.
Little Mouse," she cried,
"I love you."

Mother Mouse hugged
and kissed Little Mouse.
Moose and Goose
put the roof
on the house.

Then Little Mouse hugged
and kissed Moose and Goose.
Mother Mouse thanked them
for being so kind.

"Goodbye, Mouse," said Goose,

"my good friend Mouse."

"Goodbye, Mouse," said Moose,

"toodle-oo."

From the little red roof
on the little red house
Little Mouse waved and cried:

"Goodbye, Moose. Goodbye, Goose.
What a happy, happy thing it is,
to have a mother and to live in a house
and to be and to know
that I am a Mouse."

Ellen Raskin had designed more than 1,000 book jackets before she wrote and illustrated her first picture book for children, *Nothing Ever Happens on My Block*, which was selected as a *Herald Tribune* Prize Book, one of the *New York Times'* Ten Best of the Year, and a Notable Book by the American Library Association. Since then she has written as well as illustrated about a dozen more, including one full-length mystery novel for children, and has illustrated some twenty books for other authors. Her recent *Moe Q. McGlutch, He Smoked Too Much*—was published by Parents' Magazine Press.

Ellen Raskin was born in Milwaukee, Wisconsin, and now lives in New York City.